TWO-MINUTE LITTLE CRITTER STORIES

Eight Favorite Stories, Including *Just a Mess*,
I Just Forgot, and *Just Go to Bed*

BY
MERCER MAYER

A GOLDEN BOOK • NEW YORK
Western Publishing Company, Inc., Racine, Wisconsin 53404

JUST A MESS

Today I couldn't find my baseball mitt.
I looked in my tree house.
I looked under the back steps.

I asked Mom if she had seen it.
She said to try my room.
I never thought to look there.
What a mess!

Mom said it was time to clean
my room. So I asked her to help.
She said, "You made the mess, so
you can clean up the mess."

So I just did it myself.
First I put a few things in the closet.

I put my clothes
in the drawers.

I shut the lid
to my toy box
and put away
my books.

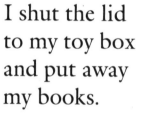

The rest of the mess could fit
under my bed, so I put it there.

I thought I might wash the floor.
But Mom said, "NO!"
So I just vacuumed instead.

Everything was just about perfect.
Then I noticed that my pillow
was missing.
I looked on the other side of my bed,
and guess what I found.
My baseball mitt.

JUST ME AND MY BABYSITTER

When Mom and Dad go out,
the babysitter comes.
My little sister cries,
but I don't.

Mom says I'm the babysitter's
big helper.
I take the babysitter's coat
and hang it in the closet.

After we have supper, I fill up the
sink and help the babysitter do
the dishes.

We give my little sister a bath.
I help her put on her pajamas.
Then we put her to bed, just
me and my babysitter.

When the work is over,
we can have some fun.

We watch a movie.
Then I go right to bed when
my babysitter tells me to.
We have a good time, just
me and my babysitter.

I JUST FORGOT

This morning I remembered
to brush my teeth, but I
forgot to make my bed.
I put my dishes in the sink
after breakfast, but I forgot
to put the milk away.

I didn't forget to feed the goldfish.
He just didn't look hungry. I'll
do it now, Mom.

I didn't forget to water the plants.
They looked fine to me.

I went outside to play in the rain.
I remembered to put on my rain slicker,
but I forgot to put on my rubber boots.

When I came inside, I had cookies and milk.
I was just going to eat three cookies, but
I forgot to count them.

When I took my bath, I remembered to wash
behind my ears.
I didn't use soap, but I didn't forget to.
I just don't like soap.

But there is one thing I never forget.

When I go to bed, I always
remember to have Mom read me
a bedtime story. And I always
remember to kiss her good night.

JUST ME AND MY PUPPY

I wanted a puppy, just for me.
So I traded my baseball mitt for one.

Boy, were Mom and Dad ever surprised!
They said I could keep him if I took care
of him myself.
So I am taking very good care of my puppy.

When I feed him
in the morning,
he eats every bite.

Then I put on his leash,
and we go for a walk.
I am teaching my puppy
how to heel.

He is learning how to stay—
except when he sees a cat.

My puppy is learning lots of tricks,
but he still needs some practice.

My puppy is a big help around the house.
He brings in the paper for my dad.
And he keeps me company
while I do my homework.

When we get ready for bed,
my puppy is always playful.
But it's fun to go to sleep
with him.

I WAS SO MAD

I wanted to keep some frogs in the bathtub,
but Mom wouldn't let me.
I was so mad.
I wanted to play with my little sister's dollhouse,
but Dad wouldn't let me.
I was so mad.

Dad said, "Why don't you play in the sandbox?"
I didn't want to do that.

Mom said, "Why don't you play on the slide?"
I didn't want to do that, either.
I was too mad.

I wanted to practice my juggling show instead.
But Mom said, "No, you can't."
Was I ever mad.

"You won't let me do anything
I want to do," I said.
"I guess I'll run away."
That's how mad I was.

So I packed my wagon
with my favorite toys.
And I packed a bag of cookies
to eat on the way.

Then I walked out the front door.
But my friends were going
to the park to play ball.
I wanted to go, too.
Mom said I could.

I'll run away tomorrow
if I'm still so mad.

JUST MY FRIEND AND ME

I asked Mom if I could have a friend over,
'cause I just don't want to play alone.
There are so many things we can do—
just my friend and me.

First we climb the apple tree.
I could climb higher if I really wanted to.

Then we have a jump rope contest.
My friend jumps a hundred times.
I could do that…

but sometimes I like to let my friend win.

We take turns playing daredevil on my new bike.
My friend tries to stand on the seat.
It's only bent a little.
I bet Dad can fix it.
My mom takes care of our cuts and bruises.
My friend cries a lot.
I only cry a little.

After we finish playing, we pick up my toys
and put them away. My friend says he'll put
away the comic books.

When my friend's mom comes to
pick him up, we say good-bye.
We always have fun when it's
just my friend and me...
but sometimes it's great
just to be all alone.

WHEN I GET BIGGER

When I get bigger, I'll be able to do lots of things. I'll go to the corner store by myself and spend my allowance on anything I want.

I'll wait until the light is green. Then I'll look both ways for cars before I cross the street.

I'll have my own watch,
and I'll tell everyone
what time it is.

I'll go on a bus to
Grandma and Grandpa's.
And I'll go to first grade.

When I get bigger, I'll have
a real leather football, my
own radio, and a pair of
super-pro roller skates.

I'll have a two-wheeler
and a paper route.
I'll make lots of money.

When I get bigger, I'll camp out
in the backyard all night long.

Or I'll stay up to see the end of the late movie.
Even if I get sleepy, I won't go to bed.

But right now I have to go to
bed, because Mom and Dad
say I'm not bigger yet.

JUST GO TO BED

I'm a cowboy and I round up cows.
I can lasso anything.
Dad says, "It's time for the
cowboy to come inside and get
ready for bed."

I'm a general and I have
to stop the enemy army
with my tank.
Dad says, "It's time for
the general to take a bath."

I'm a space cadet and I
zoom to the moon.
I capture a robot with
my ray gun.
Dad says, "This giant
robot has captured the
space cadet and is going
to put him in the tub
right now."

After my bath, I'm
Super Critter flying
over the city.

I'm a train engineer being
chased by bandits.

Dad says, "Put on your pajamas."
But I'm a race car driver,
and I just speed away.
Dad says, "The race is over.
Now put on these pajamas
and just go to bed!"

Well, maybe a tired bunny
could sleep in a bed...
just this once.